W9-AKE-020

America's Promise

By Alma Powell

Illustrated by Marsha Winborn

HarperCollins*Publishers*

For Bryan and Jeffrey, I promise . . .

America's Promise—The Alliance for Youth
and 🛒 *are trademarks of America's Promise—*
The Alliance for Youth, Inc. Use of these marks by permission only.

America's Promise
Text copyright © 2003 by America's Promise—The Alliance For Youth, Inc.
Illustrations copyright © 2003 by Marsha Winborn
Printed in the U.S.A. All rights reserved.
www.harperchildrens.com

Library of Congress Cataloging-in-Publication Data
Powell, Alma.
America's promise / by Alma Powell ; illustrated by Marsha Winborn.
    p.   cm.
Summary: When Honey and her little brother Benji move to a new
neighborhood, they meet Mrs. Mayberry, who has created a clubhouse so
the neighborhood children have a safe place to play.
Includes factual information about America's Promise—The Alliance for
Youth, Inc.
ISBN 0-06-052172-4 — ISBN 0-06-052173-2 (lib. bdg.)
[1. Neighborhood—Fiction.] I. Winborn, Marsha, ill. II. Title.
PZ7.P777 Am   2003   [E]—dc21   2002010272

Typography by Jeanne L. Hogle
1 2 3 4 5 6 7 8 9 10
❖
First Edition

America's Promise

AMERICA'S PROMISE—The Alliance for Youth—was founded in 1997 to challenge the nation to make our children a national priority.

Our mission is to mobilize people from every sector of American life to build the character and competence of our nation's youth by fulfilling five promises for young people:

1. CARING ADULTS IN EVERY CHILD'S LIFE

Develop relationships with parents, tutors, mentors, coaches, and other adults with an interest in the child's well-being.

2. A SAFE PLACE AFTER SCHOOL

Create locations with structured activities during nonschool hours.

3. A HEALTHY START

Provide good nutrition, protective immunizations, and sound dental care and hygiene.

4. MARKETABLE SKILLS

Offer effective education and practical experiences for career development.

5. OPPORTUNITIES TO GIVE BACK

Encourage community service—so that the cycle continues.

Over five hundred organizations and communities across the nation have pledged to fulfill these promises.

Americans working together for a brighter future—this is *our* promise to the promise of America, her children.

—ALMA POWELL

"Benji, come on!"
That's my mom.

"My wagon's stuck."
That's my brother, Benji. He won't go anywhere without his little red wagon.

We just moved, and Momma is starting a new job. We're going to a day-care center until she can find a baby-sitter.

Just for a few days, Honey.

Do we have to go to the baby day-care center, Momma?

As we turn a corner, we see a bunch of kids sitting on a stoop. There's a girl my age, a boy who looks a little older, and a couple of little kids like Benji.

"Hey. Are you new around here?" asks the girl.

"Yes. My name's Honey."

"My name's Marigold. We were just about to go to Mrs. Mayberry's. Do you want to come along?"

Who's Mrs. Mayberry?

Marigold explains that Mrs. Mayberry lives down the block. "She used to be a teacher, only now she's tired."

"You mean *retired*!" says a boy named Justin. "Mrs. Mayberry told our folks that our street was too dangerous for us to play in, and she was going to do something about it. So now we play in her house."

Honey, take good care of your brother.
I'm counting on you today.

Okay, Momma.

Momma says she has already heard great things about Mrs. Mayberry's Play and Learn House. She calls Mrs. Mayberry to introduce us and find out if we can visit. She tells me I have to take Benji too.

AMERICA'S PROMISE Every child will have a caring adult in their life.

We set off. "But first we have to stop and get Melvin," Marigold tells me.

Inside the corner store, a teenager named Melvin waves at Marigold and tells his uncle, Mr. King, that he's finished.

As we fill up Benji's wagon, Melvin tells me that he works at his uncle's store every Saturday. I ask him if he misses playing with his friends.

"Sometimes," he says. "But it's worth it. I'm learning to be careful and get things right. And that's important for an accountant."

After we meet Mrs. Mayberry, we discover all sorts of great stuff to do.

At first Benji sticks close by me, but pretty soon Mrs. Mayberry gets him to come over and read a book. Can you believe she has a book about a little red wagon?

The Mayberry Community
Play and Learn
House

READING!

IT'S THE WAY TO FLY!

AMERICA'S PROMISE All children deserve safe places to learn in and play.

Marigold teaches me to play checkers on this board made completely out of wood. She says it was Mr. Mayberry's before he died.

I've just won my first-ever game of checkers when Mrs. Mayberry appears from the kitchen with a big bowl in her arms. She cut up all the apples and oranges and made a fruit salad.

AMERICA'S PROMISE Every child will have a healthy start that includes nutritious food, medical care, and exercise.

After our snack, Mrs. Mayberry goes over to an old record player. She flips a switch and music comes out. It's jazz like my uncle Jesse plays on his saxophone.

"HI DEE, HI DEE, HI DEE, HO," the man on the record calls out, and all the kids sing it with him. Justin pretends like he's playing the saxophone. Marigold and I dance around till we fall on the floor laughing.

As we pick ourselves up, there's a knock at the door.

"Who is it?" calls Mrs. Mayberry.

"Mayor Crawley," says a booming voice.

The mayor runs the entire city. Why would he be coming here?

When Mrs. Mayberry opens the door and the mayor comes in, the room shrinks. He's a big, tall man with a friendly smile and a voice that sounds like my favorite uncle—that's Uncle Jesse.

Mayor Crawley tells us about a new place to play.

SAFETY COUNTS!

SAFE TIPS:

FIRST AID

The Mayor!

Wow!

"But you can't play there yet," says Mayor Crawley. "It's only an empty lot." He explains that before the lot can become a park, the city has to clean it up to make it safe for children.

"Why don't we clean up the lot? We could do it right now!" says Marigold.

Whoa, now! That's nice of you to offer, but it's a lot of work. It's not like playing; it's like having a job.

"Come on, Mr. Mayor, let us do it," I plead.

The mayor tugs his beard and looks at Mrs. Mayberry. "What do you think?"

Mrs. Mayberry looks the mayor right in the eye. "These children know an opportunity when they see one, sir. If they put their minds to it, they can do the job."

All right. Let's go see it.

We all get a ride in the mayor's car. But when we jump out, I feel my heart drop to the pit of my stomach. The lot is full of everything you can imagine.

Volunteer for America

This isn't an empty
It's a garbage dur

"Everybody can be great
because anybody can serve."
Martin Luther King Jr.

"Nobody said it was going to be easy," says the mayor. Then Melvin says, "Mrs. Mayberry always tells us, 'If you think you can or you think you can't, you're probably right.'"

I turn to the mayor and say, "Sir, we're ready to work."

The grass is taller than Benji.

The mayor drives away and comes back with all the tools we need: trash bags, gloves, rakes, even an old lawn mower. He has to go down to City Hall, but he'll be back later to check on us.

We pick up all the rocks, bricks, pipes, and trash. We load them into Benji's wagon and wheel them off to the side of the road. The big kids take turns cutting the grass.

Benji and the little kids work hard too. The gloves they wear are so big, they almost cover their entire arms.

My dad showed me how to use this kind of mower!

Just when we're all starting to get hungry, Mr. King, Melvin's uncle from the store, comes by in his car. He's got a box full of sandwiches and juice for us. That food sure tastes good!

25

After lunch, we get back to work. Finally, five hours
after we started, the lot looks much better, except for a big rock.
  At first Marigold and I try to move it. It won't budge.
Then we ask all the little kids to help. That doesn't work either.
  Just then the mayor pulls up in his car.
He can't believe all the work we've done.
But there's one problem—the big rock.

This is fantastic.
You finished it!

We haven't finished anything
unless we can move that rock

The mayor is a real big man. And he's real smart, so he bends down to use his legs and back. He says, "Heave HO!"

The rock comes off the ground. The mayor pushes harder. But he can't tip it over. He looks at us with a disappointed face.

I stare at the ground and kick a clump of newly cut grass.

"You did your best, children," says Mrs. Mayberry.

"That's right," says the mayor. "The human body can only take us so far, and then we need machines to finish the job. I have an idea." He walks over to one of the bags and pulls out a long metal pipe.

He points to an old cinder block. "Bring that over to the rock."

Marigold and I follow his directions.

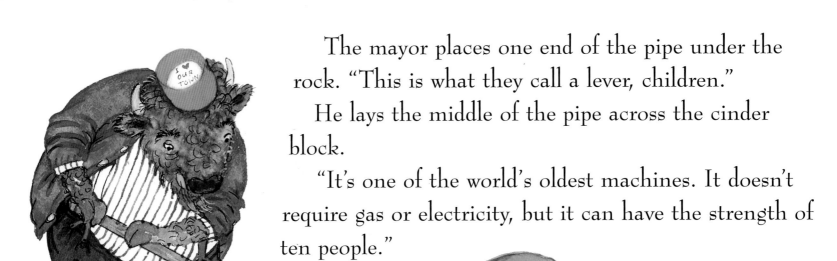

The mayor places one end of the pipe under the rock. "This is what they call a lever, children."

He lays the middle of the pipe across the cinder block.

"It's one of the world's oldest machines. It doesn't require gas or electricity, but it can have the strength of ten people."

The mayor pushes down on the pipe.
Easily the pipe lifts the rock up and up and up until it rolls over!

Yeah!
It's working!

The rock rolls over and over until it comes to rest upside down near the edge of the lot. The mayor smiles proudly. "Sometimes when strength isn't enough, you have to use your brains."

"Yes, sir, but even with a lever you won't be able to put that big rock in your car and take it away," says Melvin.

"No," says the mayor, "but I think that's all right. 'Cause look! Someone else is using his brains too."

"Let's just leave it here," Benji says. "For kids who get tired of playing and need to take a nap."

We all laugh. Then we help the mayor load his car with the trash and tools.

We wave as the mayor drives away.

Benji is pretty funny sometimes.

When he's out of sight, I turn away and start thinking about home. Everyone is ready to go except Benji. He's still looking off down the street where the mayor drove away.

Do you think I could be like him when I grow up someday?

Yes. I promise.